WHY ALWAYS ME?

Omoruyi Uwuigiaren

WHY ALWAYS ME?

FICTIONALL

Chapter One - Hard Times

Tom wore a long face and trudged on. His trousers had faded and clothed with dust. Reaching the threshold, he inserted the key into the lock and embraced his house. He hissed and slammed the door behind him, for the evening was the worst day of his life. He had to work late again even though it was Christmas Eve. But now, at last, the hammer had fallen on him! As soon as he was indoors, Tom sank into his favorite chair. After a time, he sat up and drew his rickety table. The little man lit up the room and his face looked pale in the lamplight. He took the letter out of his pocket. He lowered his bifocals. He glanced above them at the letter and a deep melancholy settled over his spirit. The company had sacked Tom and it was a bitter pill to swallow. "WHY ALWAYS ME?" he banged the table.

Tom had disposed of the letter when he heard a faint knock on the door. "Who's there?"

"It's I, Priscilla," her voice was as soft as the morning breeze.

Tom masked his anger with an exaggerated smile and opened the door. He said a friendly good evening to her. "I am sure you came to inquire why I did not attend the church service. My employer asked me to work extra hours…"

"Oh, I understand," the lady smiled as Tom led her into his humble home. Priscilla sat on a chair with her back to the wall. She placed her hands on her thighs and glanced at the little man. "I have good news for you." She revealed, "God told me that you have lost your job. But He will use this setback to turn your life around."

A ray of hope flushed over Tom's suntanned face as he sat up and muttered, "Amen!"

She closed her eyes and faced the ceiling. Priscilla brought her hands together, making recitations as if she was praying to a powerful god. Then she paused and turned to Tom. She swallowed hard and said, "The Company downsized to reduce cost…"

"Yes. The manager told me they will downsize. But I never saw this coming," Tom nodded almost a million times. "I didn't plan for it. I am confused!"

"I understand," the prophetess said. "You can bounce back. I have a secret that will make you rich. Do you want to hear?"

"Yes, oh yes!" the little man answered. He straightened his chin and looked at her face.

"You have an eighteen carat diamond ring you inherited from your father. It's wrapped up in a handkerchief in the right-hand corner of the third drawer. God said you are to get it and give it to me!"

Tom gasped and beat his chest. "Ah, my heirloom? I have never told anyone about it. How did you know I have it under my roof?"

Priscilla laughed, "God told me now. It's the spirit. Do as he had said and you will be fine!"

The little man chewed his lower lips as he imagined that his setback was temporary. He would live in luxury for the rest of his life if he turns the diamond over to Priscilla. Then he sat back and scratched his head. She was right about the diamond in the drawer, he thought. He decided to give this a try. Everything that she had said was true. As if he was under a spell, he rose to his feet and moved to the corner, and then returned to the table with the heirloom. Priscilla grabbed it and placed it in her pocket. "I like people who obey God," she smiled and gave him a hug. "If you need another hug, just ask," she heaved. "Follow me!"

"Where are we going?" Tom yawned and shifted his weight to one leg.

She rubbed her hands together. "I want to introduce you to a friend. If you have a little money, he knows how to multiply it many times over!"

Tom dreamed of the money. He said, "Thank you. I will be forever grateful, Priscilla."

Priscilla held his hand and they walked out of the house.

Chapter Two - Prophet Wusel

It was almost nightfall. They walked very fast. After covering a good distance on foot, they took a bend that led to an old, deserted street. They arrived at a building whose walls were old and crumbling. With a little push, the gate opened and they went inside. The lady carried herself to the main building. Tom was a shadow of himself. He looked pale and drawn. He ran to catch up with the young feet of Priscilla.

She made their presence felt with a gentle knock on the door. Not long after, a man of great sartorial elegance, who was shaven and had a strong square jaw, opened the door. He smelled like a bar. "I thought you said we will see tomorrow?" he asked her.

"Yes," Priscilla cocked her head. "Things changed. I brought my friend."

"Good. Only change is constant, my dear," smiled the prophet. "Come on in." As he led them into the house, he glanced at the little man with the corner of his eye. "Your name is Tom!"

Their eyes met as Tom nodded. He paused. "Wait. How did you know my name? We have never net before."

"I am a prophet of God. There is nothing hidden under the sun," Wusel replied. He moved away. "I don't need to know before I can say things about you," his voice echoed in the passage. Pricilla and Tom followed him.

As they got to the door that led to one of the rooms, the prophet paused. He turned to Tom, "My friend, a truckload of misfortune hangs from your neck like an Olympic medal! To be free, you will do yourself a lot of good if you cooperate with me."

"Yes, I lost my job!" Tom gasped. "I am not happy. I will do whatever you want me to do."

The prophet placed his hand on the door knob. "Don't worry. Weeping may endure for the night but joy comes in the morning," he commented. "If you agree to do what I ask of you, you will spend the rest of your life in complete happiness." He opened the door and went inside. Priscilla and Tom followed him.

As soon as prophet Wusel sank into a chair, he glanced up at Tom, "You are in a holy place. You should be on your knees." He frowned as if the little man had committed a crime.

Tom fell on his knees. His head bowed. He brought his hands together as tears gathered in his eyes. "Please, help me. My life is in a mess!"

The prophet sat up. He flashed an exaggerated smile at Tom. He placed his hand that was as hard as the back of a turtle on his chin and fixed his gaze on the little man. His strong square jaw made him look like a troll. Then he turned to Priscilla who smiled and back to Tom. "You will need to buy some items for prayers. By the time I am through, you will select jobs!" Wusel disclosed. He sat back and smiled. He added, "Stand up. You can make yourself comfortable on that chair." Wusel pointed to the seat in front of him.

"What do I need to buy?" Tom asked as he sat down.

Wusel leaned back in the chair. "Your case is peculiar. You need three things. A pig to stop your bad luck, a goat to fight off the evil spirits and a

11

sheep for good luck," the prophet said and sneezed. "By the time I am through, you will be rich!"

Pleased with what he had, Tom scratched his head. "How much will that cost?"

"Ah," the prophet faced the ceiling and chewed his lower lip. "At least, one hundred and fifty thousand will do!"

The little man's countenance fell because that amount was what he had saved his entire life. "That's a huge sum," he commented. "Can't we cut corners and still achieve the same result, prophet?"

"NO!" the prophet shook his head. "Your problem is like a mountain. You will be forever grateful to me after the prayers." Wusel closed his eyes and lowered his head, making recitations as if he was praying to a powerful god. Then he paused and raised his head. He flashed a menacing smile at Tom. "Your father died of cardiac arrest when you were a boy and your mother abandoned you in an orphanage…"

"You are right," Tom sat up and fixed his gaze on the prophet.

"You see. That is why you must obey God so that your father's misfortune won't hunt you down like a dog! You can run. But you cannot hide. It will find you out and cause you pain if you don't stop the nonsense."

Tom's heart of heart died within him. "I have always feared for my life. I will get the money as soon as possible."

"When?" We want to know!" Priscilla cut in.

Tom glanced at his wristwatch. "The time is far spent," he remarked. "I will be here at first light tomorrow! Can I use my credit card?"

"No. We are going to the ram market. Most of the traders are foreigners. They are not document. So they prefer to be paid in cash," said Wusel.

"No problem. I will be here as soon as possible," Tom reiterated.

"Good. Hope you can find your way from there?" asked the prophet.

"Yes," he answered.

"Ah. Good. I would have asked Priscilla to show you the way."

"There is no need," Tom said. He nodded and rose to his feet.

As he turned to go, the prophet stopped him. "Hold on. God told me something. He said in three days, you will smile!"

"Amen!" Tom said and moved away.

Priscilla followed Tom out of the room. They moved to the gate. Once Tom was out of the compound, she secured the gate. Priscilla returned to Wusel who was waiting in the room. She fell on him and gave him a million embraces. "You are a top performer!" She kissed him. "The charm is working. The witch doctor knows his job. We will have to renew it every month."

"Sure. It's worth every dime we invested!" Wusel smiled.

"And you are not doing badly as a prophet. You should act movies too."

"No, I will stick to this. Acting movies is not my life. I look like a prophet. A shepherd has a grave

13

responsibility to tend and nurture the sheep in a loving attitude. Are you sure he will come tomorrow?"

"Of, course!" She brought out the eighteen carat diamond ring that Tom gave her. "This is our reward for today!"

"It's nice!" Wusel inspected the piece and nodded his head. Then his face broke into a gap toothed smile. "How did you get this?"

"The charm worked wonders. I take it everywhere I go. As soon as I was outside his house, I put some of the powder on my lips. I entered his house and started talking. He thought it was God talking to him," she smiled and they kissed.

Wusel smiled back. "You have learned this trade. Get the men ready. We must not allow Tom to slip off our hands!"

"Okay, I will get in touch with them immediately!" They kissed.

"I will marry you. I can't let you slip off my hands. You are an important part of this business!" Wusel spoke. "We should stay together as a family."

"Alright," Priscilla kissed him. Her hand traveled from his neck to his chest.

His fingers caressed the back of her neck. They kissed on the chair for some time. She unbuttons his shirt. Wusel was hard in his pants. He touched her delicately. She moaned as his hand found its way under her body. Her skirt dropped to the ground. Wusel carried her to the table. She leaned back and spread her legs. She wanted his body inside of her. Wusel unzipped his trousers and bruised her petals.

Chapter Three - Petty Thieves

Wild and free, they could feel the heat of the sun. The money was in black polythene and Tom held it close to his chest as they faced the ram market.

There were few legs on the road as Tom followed the prophet as if he was under a spell. It was a perilous time and he was too happy to sense any danger. The end of my misery had come, he thought. Wusel walked with measured steps. He was in a world of his own and expected nothing more than success. At intervals, Wusel would glance at Tom and parade smile on his face.

There were tall buildings in rows. Their feet blanketed with dust, and the little man was under the illusion that he would get a better life. The prophet led Tom through many streets. As they approached a bend, two hefty men who wore masks jumped out of a corner. They brandished their weapons and fell on Tom and Prophet Wusel. One of the thieves knocked Tom over with a single blow and the other pinned the prophet to the ground. Panting like a terrified lizard, the little man tried to escape. But the blow that landed on his neck weighed him down. Under the weight of the thief, Tom yelled as if he had lost a vital part of his. The thief placed what seemed like a toy gun on his neck and searched Tom. He found a large sum of money. He grabbed it. They jumped on a waiting motorbike and zoomed off.

After the thieves had gone, Tom and the prophet breathed the air of salvation. The little man looked about, for his heart began to beat fast. He fell on his knees. He glanced at Wusel, "They have taken the money!" He lowered his head, banging the old earth.

Wusel crossed his arms over his body and masked his face with a frown. "It's your fault, Tom.

As you know, the world is a battlefield. You don't carry cash in the public the way you did!" he commented. "You should have hand the money over to me. But you decided to do things your way. Now it has ended badly for us. That's the price to pay for being silly!" The prophet adjusted his huge frame and moved away.

"Please wait!" Tom gathered himself up and ran after him. "What about the prayers?"

"I have no business with losers!" He raised his hands above his head and waved them. He crossed to the other side of the road and disappeared through some buildings. Tom tried to follow but lost him. Confused, Tom stood akimbo. He looked in every direction. It was hard to believe that he had lost all his savings. And the man, whom he thought was a blessing, had deserted him. His countenance fell as he faced the way home.

By the time Tom got to his street it was already evening. He heard a distant cry that almost reached the high heavens. There was pandemonium at the other side of the street but he was too far away to figure out what was wrong. The problem was grave as the evening took its place in the progression of days. Six flats, including Tom's apartment, were on fire. Little children played with matches in the kitchen and they had caught the building on fire. The flame was out of control. People wailed. Flames pierced the dark night and settled on the bosom of the wandering clouds. It took two hours to put out the fire. By the time the fire service put out the fire, there was nothing left. The inferno had gulped the building. Nobody, including Tom, could recover their effects.

Not the best of times as hopelessness sat on the throne of his heart. Tom ran from one end of the building to the other to see if he could savage his effects. Hard times had struck and swept Tom off his feet. Finally, all that he had was gone, including the roof over his head. As the boughs of trees danced and bowed to the sweet movement of the evening breeze, Tom moved to the shadows. He leaned on a wall where he had the luxury of crying.

After a time, he raised his head and wiped his face with the back of his hand. He thought of visiting Wusel, but it was rather too late to embark on the journey. As he pondered where to pass the night, an idea flew into his head. Down the street was a school. I can pass the night there, he thought. Then he carried himself to the school. As the little man knocked on the gate, a mean face peered down from a little opening on the gate. "Yes, what can I do for you?" the voice asked.

Tom adjusted. He glanced up at the man and stammered, "Sir, I need your help!"

The guard chuckled. "You need my help? Are you sure you are in the right place? This is a school. Not a charity!"

The little man rubbed his hands together, "I need a place to pass the night…"

The guard hissed and raised an eyebrow. "You are funny. This place is not a hotel. Go to the town…There is a hotel across the road. You can go there and pass the night."

"Fire gulped my house and I lost everything," he managed to croak as tears gathered in his eyes.

"Ah," the guard looked at Tom. "So you lived in that house? I saw the building go up in flames!" He shook his head. "It's a pity. I would have loved to help you for a night but I am only a guard here. It's difficult." He turned to go. "There are things I cannot do. I could be biting my own fingers."

"WAIT! I will leave at first light! I promise!"

The guard returned, "Don't put me in trouble. This is where I get my daily bread."

Tom fell on his knees and placed his hands together. "Please, I promise. I will leave very early and I won't come back!"

The guard paused and observed the little man discreetly. Tom was in a dilemma and then he decided to help the poor soul. The guard opened the gate halfway. He looked about to make sure that no eye was watching and then turned to Tom. "Don't let me wake you up tomorrow, little man. The school authorities must not see you. They will query me for letting you in without their permission. I could lose my job!" He swallowed hard and chewed his lower lip. "Come in!" As Tom walked in, he locked the gate. He placed his club on the shoulder and turned to Tom. "Come with me!" They moved to the back of the school where he offered Tom a couch to pass the night.

The little man was pleased with his new friend as he thanked him almost a thousand times. But as the guard went back to his post, Tom sat on the couch with hand to chin, gazing at the wandering clouds.

Sad memories invaded his head and he could not sleep.

After a time, the guard returned to his side with two glasses and a bottle of wine. He sat beside the little man. "I know you will find it hard to sleep, my friend. Do you have a name?"

The little man nodded and said, "Tom."

"Tom? That sounds nice." The guard adjusted, he raised his head and faced the heavens. He placed his hand on Tom's shoulder, "I am Baldwin. Listen, life is no bed of roses. Do me a favor, Tom. Put your sad times on the doorstep of the past. To be reborn or die is your choice," he smiled. "Come on, let's drink." He handed Tom a wine glass and filled it with wine.

The hospitality was great. He grabbed the drink with both hands and emptied it into his belly. He belched and their eyes met. "Thank you. It's a sweet wine." Tom stretched the glass to him for more. He poured more drinks.

"I once had a family," the guard commented. "But I lost them in a road accident. My wife and child have gone to meet our ancestors. Now I am left to spend the rest of my life alone. We live in a cruel world. Do you agree?" He looked at the little man.

"Yes, but you can still remarry," he said.

The guard nodded, "I will but it is expensive to raise a decent family!"

Tom smiled. "I will get over my problem."

He raised his head. "It's a great thing to bend any circumstance to your favor." The guard rose to his feet, he placed the bottle of wine beside Tom. "You have the drink. Let me check the compound to see if there is any trouble." He flashed his torchlight at the bottle of wine and walked away.

"Thank you," Tom spoke. He watched the guard disappear into the warm hands of the night. Not long after, weariness weighed upon the little man, and he knew he must get some rest to face the morning. He climbed onto the couch and put the day behind him.

Back in the building. Wusel, Pricilla and the thieves were in one of the rooms. The money they stole from Tom was the center table. It was all set up by the prophet. They shared the money amid drinking and eating. After having a good time together, they gathered their effects and moved them into a pickup truck outside of the house. Wusel and his cohorts moved into the shadows.

Chapter Four - Grace to Grass

Next day, the morning walked into brightness. Tom rushed out of the school and dashed to the prophet's house. He thought Wusel and Priscilla could save him from his catastrophe. Immediately he got to the building, he fell on the gate and banged it hard.

There was no response.

He called their names.

There was no answer.

His shoulders sagged. He sank on the floor and lowered his head. Not long after, a minivan pulled up in front of the house. A man in the pool of old age alighted from the van and moved to the gate. As he inserted the key into the hole, he noticed the little man whom he thought was fast asleep by the side. "What is he doing here?" the man wondered. Then he left the key in the hole and moved nearer. He tapped the little man on the shoulder. Tom jumped to his feet. Thinking that the old man was Wusel. He fell on him and cried, "Prophet, help me! Fire gulped my house last night!"

"I am not Wusel. Get your hands off me!" the old man yelled and shoved him off. Tom lost his balance and fell on the floor. "You smell like a bar! Listen, you can never be useful if you are always drunk. Now get the hell out of here!"

Tom thought he was in dreamland. He wiped his face with the back of his hands and looked at the man again. When he realized that the old man was not Wusel, he rose to his feet, "I am sorry sir. I thought you were Prophet Wusel."

"Wusel doesn't live here anymore. He was here until yesterday. I served him quit notice some months ago. As you can see, this building is begging for renovation!" the old man explained and turned to the gate. "I want to renovate the property."

Tom moved nearer. "Sir, Prophet Wusel was here yesterday…"

He looked at Tom with the corner of his eye. "He must have swindled you. Wusel is a clown!" He swallowed hard and added, "His notice expired last week. But he begged for a few more days to move his effects. Last night, he called to inform me that he was gone."

"Ah! Do you know where he moved to?"

"I don't know!" He opened the gate and went in.

Tom followed him into the compound.

The old man took some steps and paused. He turned to Tom. "Didn't you hear me? I said Wusel doesn't live here anymore! He moved last night!"

"I can't believe it." Tom shook his head. "This can't be true."

The old man hissed. "Don't be silly! You can check the building if you want..."

Tom ran into the house. The old man shook his head. He grinds in grief and follows Tom into the house. Tom moved straight to the room where they had met a while ago. But there was nobody. He checked the other rooms. Wusel was not only gone, all the effects in the house had gone too. Shattered, the little man beat his chest and gasped. He moved to a corner of the house, he sat on the floor and wept. As he cried, the old man walked in. He leaned on the door and crossed his arms over his body. "It is regrettable that Wusel did not tell you that he had moved. Do you have his mobile number?"

Tom glanced up at the old man with eyes flooded with tears, "No. I trusted him with all my life. So I didn't bother to ask."

He chuckled. "That is not good enough. I used to have his number. But I deleted it the moment he moved out of here. If I may ask, why do you want to see him?"

Sobbing, Tom rose to his feet. He felt disgruntled. "Since you don't have his number, there is no need to tell you what that man did to me." He walked out of the room and made for the exit.

His money and heirloom are gone. He had promised Baldwin that he would not return to the school. Tom carried himself out of the gate. He stood beside the road to ponder where to go. There was no clear destination in sight. He didn't want to go back to where he slept last night. He could cost Baldwin his job. He decided to take a walk. He could find somewhere else to pass the night.

Along the road was a deserted bungalow, which was almost overrun with bushes. The landlord abandoned the house. During the rainy season it was always flooded. The little man stopped at the building. It was the only place that came to his head. He looked about to make sure that no eye was watching and went into the house.

The rooms were cold and quiet, and overrun with rodents. The walls were dusty. Tom chose a corner. The battle for survival has begun.

Chapter Five - Different Strokes

Rosaline was stranded after work. Her driver was stuck in traffic. But he telephoned that he may not make it to pick her at the office before six o'clock in the evening. So, Rosaline packed a few things in her bag and left. The fat jolly woman had to cover a huge distance with her pair of legs. When Rosaline emerged from the evening's shadow, she did not see a robber that was lying in ambush. Like any thief, he took cover like a militia in the woods. He knew that his prey would come along shortly. The lady was eager to get home. She did not see the machination against her soul. She maneuvered her legs through the dusty and deserted street. Rosaline would have seen the robber when he came out to see if a victim was on the way. She missed the little detail because her mind was somewhere.

As Rosaline got close, the robber emerged from the bush and fell upon her. They had a fair struggle as his blow cut through her shoulder. Rosaline yelled and her bag fell into the bush. She managed to break free and bolted. She fled with her legs almost reaching the back of her head. The thief checked the nearby bush for the bag but could not find it. His few minutes of assault had yielded no result. Frustrated, the man fled into the night.

Tom was on the veranda of the bungalow when he heard the lady cry. He rose to his feet and stole on silent feet to the scene. He wanted to intervene but feared it could expose him to the thief and put his life at risk. After the thief had gone, he flashed his torchlight and came out of his corner. He moved to the scene, looking about. Not long after, he stumbled on a bag. He raised his head and looked in every direction. There was nobody at sight. Tom grabbed the bag and maneuvered himself back to the building. Happy that he was safe, he sat on the floor and opened the bag. "MONEY!" His eyes and mouth widened in surprise and his jaws dropped. The bag contained large sums of money, a mobile phone and some documents. Tom was only concerned about the money. "It appears providence has smiled on me," he thought, nodding his head as he inspected further.

Tom grabbed a bundle and smelled it. Chewing his lower lip, his heart began to beat fast. He removed some money from the bag; he rushed to a corner and hid them in a small box. As he returned, he remembered he had not eaten dinner. He took some notes from the bag and decided to visit the food vendor on the next street. But he realized it was rather too late to make such a move. The food vendor must have closed and gone home. Tom regretted that he could not eat a good meal that night. All night the little man thought of how he would spend the money to rent a house and move away from the incomplete bungalow.

The next day, the phone rang and Tom opened his eyes upon the light of the world. He crawled to where he kept the bag and grabbed the piece. He sat up and glanced at the phone. "What do I do now? If I answer this call, I stand the risk of losing everything. I must think so that I don't do something silly." The little man scratched his head. He switched off the phone and dropped it in the bag. He crawled back to the mat and lay with his face to the wall.

After a time, Tom rose from the mat looking resolved to follow the path of good men. He moved to the corner and returned the money he had kept away into the bag and switched on the phone. Not long after, the phone rang again. "Yes, who are you?" Tom answered the call. The caller identified herself as the owner of the phone and the bag, and narrated to Tom how she misplaced them. Then Tom asked the lady to meet him by four o'clock in the evening at the same junction where she was robbed.

Chapter Six - Good Samaritan

Tom had dozed off when the lady and four hefty policemen arrived at the scene. They called her phone. It rang but there was no answer. One of the police officers suggested that they check the bungalow. They could find a lead. His instinct was right. They walked inside the bungalow. They looked about and found the little man in a corner with the bag wrapped under his arm and asleep. "That's my bag!" the lady whispered to the men.

One of the officers stepped forward and tapped Tom on the shoulder. The little man stormed out of sleep. His heart sank when he saw the policemen. He threw the bag at them and fell to his knees, with hands held out and palms up. "I found the bag moments after a woman was attacked yesterday! I don't know the attacker!"

The lady rushed forward and picked up the bag. She checked if her belongings were safe. "Thank you, little man," she told Tom and placed her hand on her chest. She heaved a sigh of relief. "My things are safe." She pulled Tom to his feet. "Where do you live?" she smiled.

But the little man lowered his head, for he was reluctant to disclose. "Oh, don't worry about me. I don't have…" he paused. He swallowed hard.

The lady and the officers exchanged glances. Something was wrong but they could not put a finger on it. So the lady cleared her throat, "You are one in a million. I want us to be friends. We like to know where you live!"

"Me?" Tom raised his head. "Well, I don't have a house. It's odd but that's the truth!"

One of the officers grabbed him by the neck, "My friend, you better cooperate. Do you know who is talking to you? Take her to your house or we will make life difficult for you!"

Tom feared he would be arrested. He cried, "Please, let me go. Don't arrest me for a crime I did not commit." He glanced about, "I live here!"

Their eyes traveled from one end of the house to another and then they looked at one another. "You mean you live in that house? This is an incomplete building." the lady said.

"Yes!" The little man nodded.

"I don't believe you!"

"Well, this is the truth. Why should I lie to you?"

The officer unhandled Tom. He adjusted his old dress and sat in a corner.

His guests were shocked that a human lived in such a creepy kind of place. The place was stuffy and blanketed in dust. She looked at Tom and shook her head. "What are you doing here?" she sighed. "This is horrible. Do you have a name?"

"Yes, Tom!" The little man lowered his head in shame.

"We need to talk. You can't stay here. Will you come with me?"

Tom chuckled. "You have nothing to lose if we discuss it here."

"I agree. But for convenience, come with me. You must not fear me. I will not hand you over to the police!"

Tom looked at the lady and the officers again. He was not sure of what would happen to him. Considering the trouble that he had faced, he decided to give this a chance. He followed them.

As soon as they left the building, she discharged the police men and led Tom into her car. The little man was comfortable in the passenger seat as they drove away. After driving for thirty minutes, they pulled up in front of a hotel. She alighted and asked Tom to follow her. As they walked, she disclosed, "You will be here until I make the necessary arrangements to get you a better place. Don't panic. This hotel belongs to my father. I have enough hands to take care of you."

Tom was short of words as she led him into one of the rooms. She left and promised to come back the next day. Shortly after the lady had gone, Tom heard a faint knock on the door. He opened the door and a lady walked in with shirts and trousers. She handed the clothes to the little man. "They are from my boss," she smiled.

As Tom received them, the lady stared at him, "How did you meet her?" she asked.

"We are friends," Tom laughed. He checked the clothes.

"You are fortunate. Her father is a wealthy politician and she is his only child!"

"Only child?" Tom threw the clothes on the bed and turned to the waitress.

"Yes." The lady smiled. "It appears she likes you. She is very generous. Be good. You will enjoy my boss." Then she turned to go.

"WAIT!"

"What?" She frowned and raised an eyebrow that gave birth to a furrow on her forehead.

Tom shifted his weight to one leg and straightened his chin. "Do you have a good meal?"

"Yes," she nodded. "We have enough food for you!" Her voice was as soft as a whisper. She slammed the door and moved away.

Lost in his thought, Tom stood and stared at the ceiling. After a time, he walked to the bed to check the clothes. They were nice but he will need more than that to embrace complete happiness again.

Chapter Seven - Rosaline

Tom had a long night's rest and he could not remember the last time he tasted such sleep. Rest is a beautiful thing. Only those who know it's worth would grab it with both hands. There was a knock on the door. Tom rolled out of bed and attended to the fellow. It was his new friend. "Good morning, Madam," Tom greeted with a bow.

She laughed. "Don't bow to me," she pushed his head. "Call me Rosaline. How was your night?" She walked in with a serving girl who brought Tom's breakfast. The girl placed the meal on the table and left.

"It was great," Tom smiled. He sat on the bed with a bare chest that could only boast of a few beards, and they were like monuments on a vast land. "I did not expect you so early," Tom said and their eyes met. He rose to his feet and moved to the window. He pushed the blind and leaned on the wooden frame.

Rosaline chuckled. Her long braid almost covered half of her face. She pushed it to her shoulder, walked to the bed and sat down. "I have an appointment in an hour's time. But I don't know anything about my new friend."

The little man smiled. He returned to the bed and sat beside her. "I will summarize this in a few words."

"I am listening," said Rosaline.

Tom cleared his throat. He said, "Wits and might are far too irrelevant to be deliverance for anyone," Tom commented. "Moreover, it takes more than human discretion to survive in this part of the world. It is a tragedy to remain in a world you cannot control and all the more tragic if you do not have control over your own life. People, who surrendered the leadership of their lives, are always at the mercy of those they serve. Such was my tale." He coughed and sat up.

She laughed. "I don't understand you, Tom."

"Okay. I will make my points clear. I have suffered too much. My ordeal is an adventure I would have avoided if I had not acted foolishly. That was my downfall. My experience over the cause of time has helped me become a better man. After I lost my job, I ran into two friends, Wusel and Priscilla. They tried to help me but things didn't work out and we lost contact. They were ready to put a smile on my face. If I had them around, I am sure we would not have met. But this is the work of providence. Wusel was a man of innocence, and he was a clairvoyant. One day, we were going to the ram market. Thieves attacked us and made away with all the money I had. As for Wusel, they beat him up. That same day, fire razed my house. I spent that night in a school, and the days that followed in this bungalow." Tom paused at last.

"That's quite a story. So where is Wusel?" Rosaline asked.

"That man of innocence. Wusel encourages me. He was bold and tough. He relocated after the ordeal we had with the thieves. That was how we lost contact."

"It's unfortunate he left without your notice," she sighed. "I will be going for dinner this evening. Will you come with me?" she smiled.

"I will," Tom returned.

She looked at her wrist watch. "I am late. We will have enough time to discuss about me at dinner." She rose to her feet and gave Tom a hug and a wet kiss on his cheek. "Take care of yourself." She smiled and walked away.

Tom followed the lady to the door and slammed shut the door. After she had gone, he returned to the table and ate his breakfast.

Chapter Eight - The Dinner

The sky was heavy with the promise of rain when a vehicle rolled into a house at Maxwell Street. Rosaline and Tom alighted. They exchanged pleasant looks and smiles. Tom adjusted his French suit and carried himself with the lady into the mansion. There were servants at the passage to welcome the guests into the luxurious home. The little man walked like a god. He occasionally waved his hands at the pleasant faces that stood at every corner in the mansion. They were adorable. Tom enjoyed the festivities.

The table was set as they went into a large room. It was a marble floor. The curtains were beautiful and the walls shone like the gate of heaven. A man in the pool of old age and his fat jolly wife were at the table. They smiled as if they were king and Queen of a prosperous nation. "We have been expecting you, Rosaline and your guest. Please have your seats!" said the old man.

As they sat down, Rosaline cleared her throat and said, "Dad, this is the young man I told you about."

The man raised his head. He lowered his bifocals and looked above them, "Oh, the good man!"

Rosaline patted the little man on the back. "He's such a nice man, Mum, Dad."

"Good evening sir," Tom greeted with a bow.

"Welcome, young man. My daughter told me so much about you and we are happy to meet you, Tom. Thank you for preserving the documents in the bag. They are very important to this family." The man continued, "I never knew that people like you still exist. Well, my family has decided to appreciate your kind gesture. Can you work with me? I have an oil company in need of an honest manager. Please, don't say no."

Tom smiled, "Thank you, sir. I will work with you sir."

"Good," the man smiled. "You will resume next week! By the way, my daughter will discuss other issues with you." Then he turned to the attendant, "Please serve us food and drink!"

"Yes sir," the attendant bowed. He poured sweet wine and served enough pork meat and white rice, and they feasted into the night.

The evening was the best day of Tom's life. After the dinner, Rosaline took him to a bar within the premises. They were alone in the dark as the breeze blew. The night was quiet and the stars were hidden under the wandering clouds.

"The night is cold," Rosaline spoke with a voice that was as soft as a whisper. She poured out drink into her glass and sent it down her throat. She belched and slammed the glass on the table as if she was drunk.

Tom was comfortable as the lord of the night. He filled her empty glass with more wine. "Yes. It appears it will rain," he said.

Rosaline looked at the fortunate soul and threw out a question, "Have you ever fallen in love?"

Tom drank a glass and giggled. "Yes!"

"When was that?"

"Today!"

She laughed. "You are funny!"

Tom breathed, "Today is the best day of my life!"

Rosaline shook her head. She poured the little man more drink and asked, "I know what I am about to say doesn't sound nice. But I have to say it. Will you marry me?"

Tom paused. He stared at the woman. Then he returned his gaze to the glass of wine on the table. He grabbed the glass and emptied the sweet wine into his stomach. He sat up. "I was about to ask you. But I don't want you to see me as a gold digger. I should be the one proposing to you. Rosaline, will you marry me?" He grinned from ear to ear.

"Yes, I fell in love with you the very moment I set my eyes on you!" Rosaline laughed. Tom rose to his feet. He pushed the table aside. He walked to her side and fell on her. Tom gave Rosaline a million embraces. They slept at the mansion that night. The little man and Rosaline started a new life together and Tom could never be happier.

Chapter Nine - Caught in the Act

Moses owned a palatial home and several expensive cars. He was a very successful businessman. He was worth millions in cash. He had several servants, a private jet, and his children drove expensive cars. But he started going to a so-called prophet and his associate, Wusel and Priscilla. He consulted them for direction and before he would make any business deal. One day, Moses was to buy a rubber plantation and he invited the prophet to his house. "I am confused about this deal and it is worth millions."

"What business?" Wusel asked with a tight lip.

"It's a plantation owned by my friend, Fred. He lives on house eight at South End Street…"

"STOP!" He closed his eyes. He raised his hands above his head and faced heaven. "God said you should buy the plantation…"

"AMEN!" Moses leaped for joy. "I knew it. I have always wanted to own that property!"

"Wait!" Wusel continued, "How much is the property worth?"

"Ah, it's very cheap. Sixty million!"

The prophet nodded. "Good, that's great."

"When will you make the payment?"

"Monday!"

"We are in a wicked world. I would like a role in the entire process."

"Ah," Moses laughed. "You are always praying. Won't that be too much for you? Combining business and the work of God is not easy."

Wusel smiled. "I understand. It's our duty to be our brother's keeper. It takes nothing away from me if I do one or two things for you."

"Oh, it's an honor." Moses was happy as they shook hands. "Thank you, Prophet Wusel. You are great. Hold on!" He jumped to his feet and rushed into his room. Not long after, he returned to the sitting room with his cheque book and a pen. He wrote a large sum of money on the cheque and handed it to the prophet. "That's for being my prophet! You can join me on Monday. Let us go to the bank together. The property owner demanded we give him cash. I wanted to give him a cheque or make a transfer. He declined. He said he needed the payment in cash. Such a terrible man. Were it not that I wanted the property at all cost, I won't do any transaction."

Wusel grabbed the cheque with both hands and he smiled. "Oh, I will be available. Thank you my friend. You have made my day." Wusel placed the cheque in his pocket. He adjusted his huge frame and announced his leave. Moses walked his visitor to the gate. As soon as he was gone, Moses slammed the gate behind him and walked to the building. He took his phone and called the police station to make arrangements for security for Monday.

Wusel rushed to his house. Priscilla was going through her old photo album when Wusel arrived. "Woman, we have a job!" he announced. "We can't miss this meal. Moses is buying a plantation on Monday. He asked me to go with him to the bank to withdraw the money. I will also follow him to the destination where he will pay the owner of the property. This is our chance to hit it big time. It's sixty million! After this mission, we will move to another country for good. And spend our lives in wealth and plenty!"

Priscilla smiled, "Schemer! I thought you said you won't defraud people again?"

"Yes, I said so," he nodded. "I cannot resist the temptation of living the rest of my life in wealth and plenty. Once we get it, we are out of town. Please, invite the guys for a meeting tonight and let's get the show on the road." He gave her a kiss. Wusel carried her and dashed to the room. He opened the door and they fell on the bed. They were wild and free.

That night, the men gathered at the Prophet's house. Wusel briefed them about the mission. They planned how to carry out the attack and share the proceeds.

On Monday, there was change of plans. Unknown to Wusel and his cohorts, Moses had hired security operatives to accompany them to the location where he will pay for the property. Moses and Wusel had hit the road when the robbers in a moving van intersected them at a junction. The security operatives following Moses repelled the attack. Wusel didn't see this coming. Moses did not reveal he will use the service of the police officer. As things spiraled out of control, the robbers abandoned the plan and tried to escape. As the driver tried to maneuver their van out of troubled waters, the van struck an electric pole. The driver died. But his cohorts jumped out of the van. They shot some bullets into the air to scare people away and they took to their heels. The security operatives shot and chased them. One of the men who had sustained bullet wounds could no longer carry on. He fell by the wayside. The security men caught him. The others escaped. The poor soul was moved to the vehicle where Moses and Wusel were waiting.

"Don't bother taking him to the station. End him now!" Wusel suggested to the police officers.

But the injured thief said to Wusel, "Master, save me. Please don't allow them to kill me. My injury did not allow me to run. I would have escaped too!"

"Who is your master? Shut up!" Wusel glared his eyes at the injured thief. He turned to one of the security operatives. He tried to collect his gun and kill the thief to cover his tracks.

The policeman resisted and shoved Wusel aside. "Who are you? You don't have the right to take my gun from me. Not to talk of kill this man," he told Wusel. He turned to the injured thief, "Do you know him?"

"Yes," the robber nodded.

Before the situation could spiral out of control, Moses intervened. "Calm down officer. The thief is talking nonsense. Wusel is a servant of God." He pointed to the thief, "This man is a criminal! I guess he is looking for someone to implicate."

Moses and Wusel wanted to enter the car. As the security operatives dragged the thief away, he shouted, "Wusel, don't do this to me. Save me! If you don't do something, I will expose you. Wusel is our leader. He sent us to kill Mr. Moses and take the money!"

"What?" Moses exclaimed. "What did you just say?" he asked the thief.

"Wusel sent us to kill you…" he reiterated.

Before Moses could blink, Wusel grabbed him by the neck. He pulled a knife from his pocket and

48

placed it on his neck. "Drop your weapons or I'll kill him!" he thundered at the officers. His eyes darted back and forth, as he began to pull Moses away into the car.

The security men tried to resist but Moses signaled them to comply. As they dropped their weapons, the injured robber slipped off their hands. He rushed forward and grabbed one of the guns. He moved to Wusel and stood by his side. To Wusel's dismay, the injured thief asked the prophet to move away from the vehicle. With a gun pointed at his head, Wusel had nothing better to do than comply. The robber secured the driver's seat in the vehicle where they kept the money. He shot Wusel on the head and he died. Glad that the money was under his nose, he ignited the engine. He shot at one of the policemen but he missed and drove off.

Moses did not know that the man he had trusted with his life was a dangerous man. Wusel lay lifeless on the bare chest of the earth. One of the police officers crossed a motorcycle and gave chase. As they went past traffic and several bends, the robber ran into trouble. A truck emerged from a bend and the driver of the truck hit the break to give way for an oncoming car at the other end. On this side of the road was the robber in full flight. By the time he applied his break, he was already too close to the truck. He ran into the monument and lay struggling for life.

The police officer who gave chase stopped by his side. He jumped down from the motorbike. He opened the boot of the car. The money was safe. He brought out his phone from his pocket and called for reinforcements. Not long after, Moses and the others arrived. They transferred the money into another car and Moses was glad he was safe.

Later on that day, Priscilla had her shower and wore white flowing garment. Holding a newspaper, she walked into the sitting room. As she sat down to read. She had barely sat down when police officers led by Moses broke into the house. "That's his cohort!" He pointed at her.

Priscilla threw the newspaper aside. She jumped to her feet and dashed through the back door. The men gave chase and got her before she could scale the fence at the backyard. They dragged her out of the compound and bundled her into a van and drove off. Priscilla was taken to the police station and there she found out what had befallen Wusel. With her, the police were able to fish out the other robbers. Pricilla, alongside her cohorts were charged to court for robbery, conspiracy and accomplice. They were sentenced to many years imprisonment. The long arm of the law had finally prevailed against them.

THE END